THE STAR

A story to help
young children
understand
foster care

By Cynthia Miller Lovell
Illustrations by Angie J. Przystas

Note from the author

As a foster parent, I was surprised by the lack of books available for younger foster children. I wrote this story book with the help of professionals to help foster children understand their experience, know that they are not alone, and have a sense of hope.

Read this book with your foster child and ask him/her lots of questions. For guidance, please consult *Questions & Activities for The Star: A handbook for foster parents*.

Cynthia M. Lovell

Special thanks to:

Carole Birch, certified social worker at Family and Children's Services Inc.; Nancy A. French, MSW, CSW, foster care and adoptions supervisor, Calhoun County Family Independence Agency; Randall Haugen, psychologist at Battle Creek Counseling Associates; Dick Lovell, my loving husband and editor; Marsha Michal-Harrison, licensing worker for children's foster care homes at Calhoun County Family Independence Agency; Mary Rossman, adoptions specialist at Calhoun County Family Independence Agency; and the foster parents and children who listened to my story and provided invaluable feedback.

Using this book in conjunction with *Questions & Activities for The Star: A handbook for foster care* is recommended.

cut here

ORDER FORM

Title	Cost per book	Number of copies you would like		Cost
The Star: *A story to help young children* *understand foster care*	$7.95	x _____	=	_____
Questions & Activities for The Star: *A handbook for foster care*	$5.95	x _____	=	_____
The Star **AND** *Questions & Activities for The Star*	$12.90	x _____	=	_____

+ 6% Sales Tax for orders shipped to Michigan	=	_____
+ Shipping & Handling: $4.50 for first book, $2.00 for each additional book	=	_____
TOTAL	=	_____

Your Name _____ Phone Number (including area code) _____

Street Address _____

City and State _____ Zip Code _____

___ Yes, please send free information on speaking/seminars by the authors.

Any comments for the authors:

For **DISCOUNTS** on large orders,
contact the author directly:
lovellbears2002@yahoo.com or (608) 238-6348

Mail Orders: Roger Owen Rossman,

THANK YOU!

Library of Congress catalog card number pending

ISBN 0-9677010-0-7

Published by
Roger Owen Rossman
163 North Avenue
Battle Creek, Michigan 49017

One evening, when the stars were starting to shine, two women came to Kit's house. They talked with Kit's mommy, who put some of Kit's clothes in a bag. Kit was scared and not sure what to think. Kit hugged her mommy. Then she had to leave with the women in their car.

One of the women told Kit that her name was Teresa. Teresa was Kit's case worker. Her job was to keep Kit safe. Teresa explained that Kit was going to a foster home. Kit listened carefully, but she still felt confused inside.

Soon they arrived at another house. Inside were
lots of people Kit did not know. The house looked and
smelled different than Kit's house. Teresa told Kit
that the grownups were Steve and Diane. They would
be Kit's foster parents, and Kit would stay with them
for awhile.

Teresa told Kit she would come back and visit. Then she left. Diane picked Kit up and hugged her. Kit hid her eyes and felt like crying.

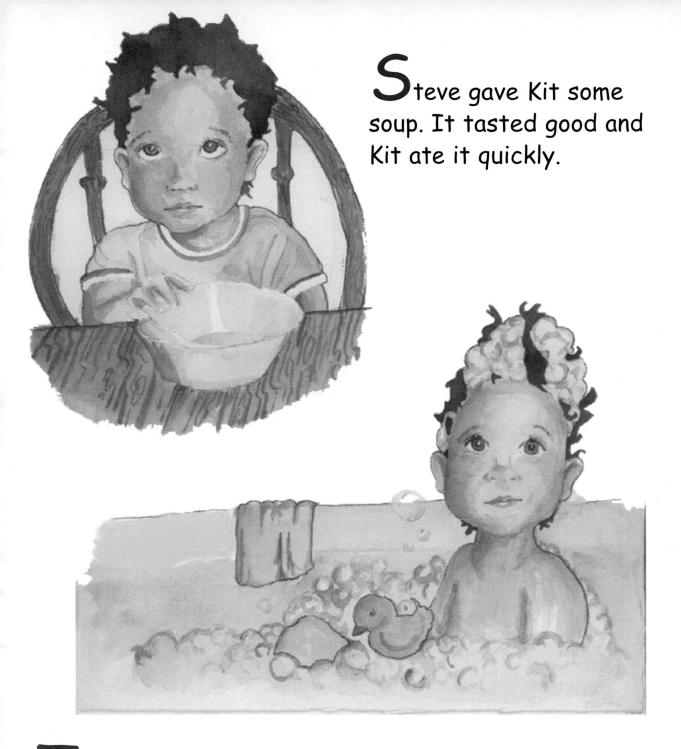

Steve gave Kit some soup. It tasted good and Kit ate it quickly.

Then, Diane gave Kit a nice, warm bath.

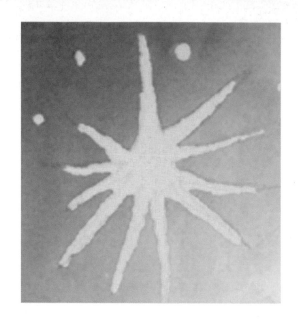

Diane tucked Kit into a soft bed. Kit felt alone and scared. She crept from her bed and looked through the window to see the stars. Kit cried. Just then, one of the stars twinkled extra bright. "It's OK, Kit, you're not alone." Kit looked up and blinked her eyes. "Who said that?" Kit looked around the bedroom. "No. Up here." Kit looked in the sky and saw the bright star. "Hi," said the star. "It's nice to meet you." "Hi," said Kit. She didn't know what to think. "I saw you crying," said the star, "and I want to help you feel better." "Nobody can make me feel better," replied Kit with a frown.

The star smiled. "Did you know there are other children like you?" "Really?" sniffed Kit. "Oh, yes," said the star. "I can see everything from up here. Why, just yesterday I saw some girls and boys go to foster homes. They are foster children, like you." "What does that mean?" Kit asked.

The star explained, "Foster children live with other families where they can be safe while their parents learn about taking better care of children." "Did the girls and boys feel scared like me?" asked Kit. "Yes," responded the star.

"You are not alone. All that you are feeling, other kids have felt, too." Kit thought about that for awhile. Then she asked, "Star, am I a foster child because I did something bad?" "Oh no," said the star. "You did not do anything wrong. You are a good and special child." Kit whispered, "Will I ever see my mommy again?"

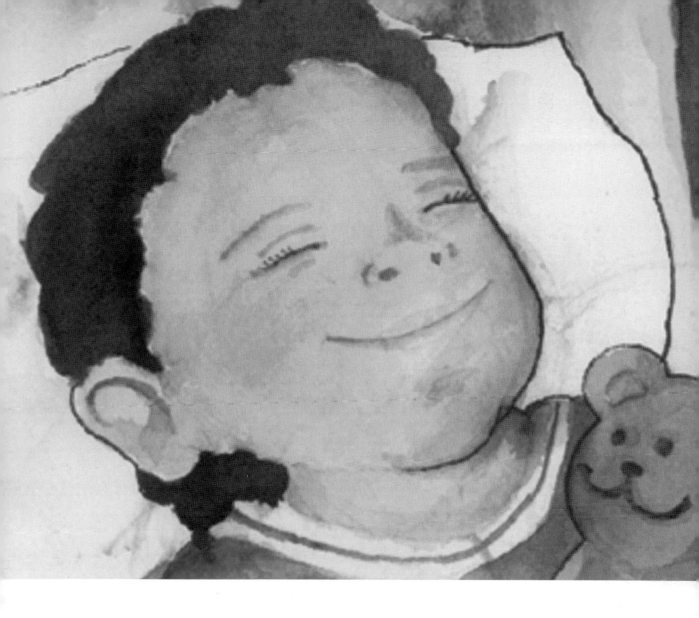

The star shone down on Kit and replied, "Maybe, but I don't have the answer right now. I do know that your foster parents will try and take good care of you. Go to bed and I'll shine for you again tomorrow night." Kit crawled back into her bed and felt better.

When Kit woke the next day, the sun was shining. She had lots of different things to get used to and explore. The days went by and Kit felt more comfortable in her new home. Each night, she told the star all she had seen and done.

Is the cat nice?
Where is the toothpaste kept?
Can I eat an apple from the table?
Can I remember all the kids' names?
Who answers the phone?

Teresa visited Kit, just as she said she would. Kit always looked forward to Teresa's visits because she would answer Kit's questions.

Kit's feelings went up and down like a roller coaster. Sometimes Kit felt happy. Sometimes Kit felt angry. Whenever Kit felt alone or sad, she looked up in the sky to find the star. Some nights she could not see the star because the clouds covered it. But she knew the star was always close by.

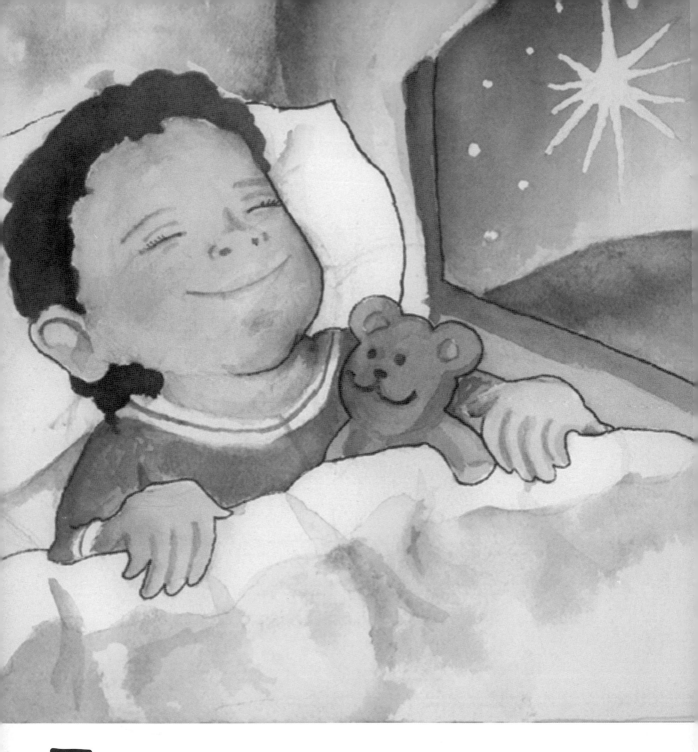

The star knows Kit will be OK, and you will be, too.